GHOST POEMS

GHOST POEMS

edited by Daisy Wallace

illustrated by Tomie de Paola

HOLIDAY HOUSE · NEW YORK

GRATEFUL ACKNOWLEDGMENT IS MADE TO THE FOLLOWING:

Columbia University Press for "Song of Two Ghosts" from *R. Fortune: Omaha Secret Societies,* 1932. Used by permission of Columbia University Press.

Farrar, Straus & Giroux, Inc., for "The Ghost of Caupolicán" from *In the Trail of the Wind: American Indian Poems and Ritual Orations* edited by John Bierhorst. Text © 1971 by John Bierhorst. Used by permission of Farrar, Straus & Giroux, Inc.

Harcourt Brace Jovanovich, Inc. for "Ghosts" by Harry Behn from *The Golden Hive.* Copyright © 1962, 1966 by Harry Behn. Used by permission of Harcourt Brace Jovanovich, Inc.

Michael Patrick Hearn for "The Phantom Ship." Copyright © 1979 by Michael Patrick Hearn.

X.J. Kennedy for "Whose Boo Is Whose?" Copyright © 1979 by X.J. Kennedy.

Steven Kroll for "Singing Ghost." Copyright © 1979 by Holiday House, Inc.

The Literary Trustees of Walter de la Mare and The Society of Authors as their representative for "Tillie" from *Poems for Children* by Walter de la Mare. Used by permission.

Lilian Moore for "Echo" by Sara Asheron. Used by permission of the author.

Thomas Nelson, Inc. for "Haunted" by William Mayne from *Ghosts.* Text copyright © 1971 by William Mayne. Used by permission of Thomas Nelson Inc. and Hamish Hamilton Limited.

Oxford University Press for "The Old Wife and the Ghost" from *The Blackbird in the Lilac* by James Reeves (1952). Used by permission of Oxford University Press.

Jack Prelutsky for "The Ghostly Grocer of Grumble Grove." Copyright © 1979 by Jack Prelutsky.

Martin Secker & Warburg Limited for "The Shepherd's Hut" by Andrew Young from *Complete Poems* edited by Leonard Clark. Used by permission of Martin Secker & Warburg Limited.

Scholastic Magazines, Inc. for "Teeny Tiny Ghost" by Lilian Moore from *Spooky Rhymes and Riddles.* Text copyright © 1972 by Lilian Moore. Used by permission of Scholastic Magazines, Inc.

Nancy Willard for "The Games of Night." Copyright © 1979 by Nancy Willard.

Library of Congress Cataloging in Publication Data

Main entry under title:

Ghost poems.

SUMMARY: Presents 17 poems about ghosts.
1. Ghosts—Juvenile poetry. [1. Ghosts—Poetry.
2. American poetry—Collections. 3. English poetry—Collections] I. Wallace, Daisy. II. De Paola, Thomas Anthony.
PN6110.G5G5   811′.088′0375   78-11028
ISBN 0-8234-0344-0

for all good GHOST-WRITERS...
D.W. & T. deP.

CONTENTS

GHOULIES AND GHOSTIES

From ghoulies and ghosties,
Long-leggity beasties,
And things that go BUMP in the night,
Good Lord deliver us.

ANONYMOUS

TEENY TINY GHOST

A teeny tiny ghost
no bigger than a mouse,
at most,
lived in a great big house.

It's hard to haunt
a great big house
when you're a teeny tiny ghost
no bigger than a mouse,
at most.

He did what he could do.

So every dark and stormy night—
the kind that shakes a house with fright—
if you stood still and listened right,
you'd hear a
teeny
tiny
BOO!

LILIAN MOORE

8

ECHO

Hello!
    hello!
Are you near?
    near, near.
Or far from here?
    far, far from here.
Are you there?
    there, there
Or coming this way,
Haunting my words
Whatever I say?

Halloo!
    halloooo
Listen, you.
Who are you, anyway?
    who, who, whoooo?

SARA ASHERON

9

GHOSTS

A cold and starry darkness moans
    And settles wide and still
Over a jumble of tumbled stones
    Dark on a darker hill.

An owl among those shadowy walls,
    Gray against the gray
Of ruins and brittle weeds, calls
    And soundless swoops away.

Rustling over scattered stones
    Dancers hover and sway,
Drifting among their own bones
    Like webs of the Milky Way.

HARRY BEHN

THE GHOSTLY GROCER
OF GRUMBLE GROVE

in Grumble Grove, near Howling Hop
there stands a nonexistent shop
within which sits, beside his stove
the ghostly grocer of Grumble Grove.

there on rows of spectral shelves
chickens serenade themselves,
sauces sing to salted butter,
onions weep and melons mutter,

cornflakes flutter, float on air
with loaves of bread that are not there,
thin spaghettis softly scream
and curdle quarts of quiet cream,

12

phantom figs and lettuce specters
dance with cans of fragrant nectars,
sardines saunter down their aisle,
tomatoes march in single file,

a cauliflower poltergeist
juggles apples, thinly sliced,
a sausage skips on ghostly legs
as raisins romp with hard-boiled eggs.

as pea pods play with prickly pears,
the ghostly grocer sits and stares
and watches all within his trove,
that ghostly grocer of Grumble Grove.

JACK PRELUTSKY

THE SHEPHERD'S HUT

The smear of blue peat smoke
That staggered on the wind and broke,
The only sign of life,
Where was the shepherd's wife,
Who left those flapping clothes to dry,
Taking no thought for her family?
For, as they bellied out
And limbs took shape and waved about,
I thought, She little knows
That ghosts are trying on her children's clothes.

ANDREW YOUNG

14

ON A TIRED HOUSEWIFE

Here lies a poor woman who was always tired,
She lived in a house where help wasn't hired:
Her last words on earth were: "Dear friends, I am going
To where there's no cooking, or washing, or sewing,
For everything there is exact to my wishes,
For where they don't eat there's no washing of dishes.
I'll be where loud anthems will always be ringing,
But having no voice I'll be quit of the singing.
Don't mourn for me now, don't mourn for me ever,
I am going to do nothing for ever and ever."

ANONYMOUS

15

SINGING GHOST

At the circus I was watching
Two dogs and a parakeet
When a ghost appeared before me
Dancing without any feet.
"Hey," I said, "what are you doing?"
He said, "Giving you a treat."
"Look," I said, "I'm at the circus.
Don't you know you can't compete?"
He said "No, my act's the greatest,"
And he burst into a song:
Oola oola woo balloola
Oola woola woola bong.
"Stop," I said, "I'll get in trouble,
You are being such a pest."
In a moment cops appeared and
Threatened me with quick arrest.
"Come along with us," they ordered,
"Songs that interrupt won't do."
So they took me off to prison
And the singing ghost came too.

STEVEN KROLL

16

TILLIE

Old Tillie Turveycombe
Sat to sew,
Just where a patch of fern did grow;
There, as she yawned,
And yawn wide did she,
Floated some seed
Down her gull-e-t
And look you once,
And look you twice,
Poor old Tillie
Was gone in a trice.
But oh, when the wind
Do a-moaning come,
'Tis poor old Tillie
Sick for home;
And oh, when a voice
In the mist do sign,
Old Tillie Turveycombe's
Floating by.

WALTER DE LA MARE

THE OLD WIFE AND THE GHOST

There was an old wife and she lived all alone
    In a cottage not far from Hitchin:
And one bright night, by the full moon light,
    Comes a ghost right into her kitchen.

About that kitchen neat and clean
    The ghost goes pottering round.
But the poor old wife is deaf as a boot
    And so never hears a sound.

The ghost blows up the kitchen fire,
    As bold as bold can be;
He helps himself from the larder shelf,
    But never a sound hears she.

19

He blows on his hands to make them warm,
 And whistles aloud "Whee-hee!"
But still as a sack the old soul lies
 And never a sound hears she.

From corner to corner he runs about,
 And into the cupboard he peeps;
He rattles the door and bumps on the floor,
 But still the old wife sleeps.

Jangles and bang go the pots and the pans,
 As he throws them all around;
And the plates and the mugs and dishes and jugs,
 He flings them all to the ground.

20

Madly the ghost tears up and down
    And screams like a storm at sea;
And at last the old wife stirs in her bed—
    And it's "Drat those mice," says she.

Then the first cock crows and morning shows
    And the troublesome ghost's away.
But oh! what a puckle the old wife sees
    When she gets up next day.

"Them's tidy big mice," the old wife thinks,
    And off she goes to Hitchin,
And a tidy big cat she fetches back
    To keep the mice from her kitchen.

JAMES REEVES

21

THE OLD GHOST

Over the water an old ghost strode
    To a churchyard on the shore,
And over him the waters had flowed
    A thousand years or more,
And pale and wan and weary
    Looked never a sprite as he;
For it's lonely and it's dreary
    The ghost of a body to be
    That has mouldered away in the sea.

THOMAS LOVELL BEDDOES

22

THE PHANTOM SHIP

Ay, don't go down to the shore, my mates,
When the moon turns white to red,
For a silent ship, a phantom ship,
Comes pressing her crew from the dead.
She moves as swift as a shadow;
No barnacles crust her hull.
No colors wave from her masthead.
Her figurehead's naught but a skull.
So silently, so swiftly, she
Seeks sailors from dusk to dawn;
But at break of day
'Cross the waking bay,

           She's gone.

        MICHAEL PATRICK HEARN

WHOSE BOO IS WHOSE?

Two ghosts I know once traded heads
And shrieked and shook their sheets to shreds—
"You're me!" yelled one, "and me, I'm you!
Now who can boo the loudest boo?"

"Me!" cried the other, and for proof
He booed a boo that scared the roof
Right off our house. The TV set
Jumped higher than a jumbo jet.

The first ghost snickered. "Why, you creep,
Call that a boo? That feeble beep?
Hear *this*!"—and sucking in a blast
Of wind, he puffed his sheet so vast

And booed so hard, a passing goose
Lost all its down. The moon shook loose
And fell and smashed to smithereens—
Stars scattered like spilled jellybeans.

"How's that for booing, boy? I win,"
Said one. The other scratched a chin
Where only bone was—"Win or lose?
How can we tell whose boo is whose?"

X.J. KENNEDY

SONG OF TWO GHOSTS

My friend
This is a wide world
We're traveling over
Walking on the moonlight.

OMAHA INDIAN SONG

26

THE GHOST OF CAUPOLICAN

Who is this,
like the tiger,
riding the wind
with his phantom-like body?
When the oaks see him,
when the people see him,
they speak with hushed voices,
saying one to another:
"Lo, brother, there is
the ghost of Caupolicán."

ARAUCANIAN INDIAN SONG

27

HAUNTED

Black hill
black hall
all still
owl's grey cry
edges shrill
castle night.

Woken eye
round in fright;
what lurks walks
in castle rustle?

Hand cold
held hand
the moving roving
urging thing:
dreamed margin

voiceless
noiseless
HEARD
feared
a ghost passed

black hill
black hall
all still
owl's grey cry
edges shrill
castle night.

WILLIAM MAYNE

THE GAMES OF NIGHT

When the ghost comes, I don't see her.
I smell the licorice drops in her pocket.
I climb out of bed, I draw her bath.
She has come a long way, and I know she's tired.

By the light of the moon, the water splashes.
By the light of the stars, the soap leaps,
it dives, it pummels the air,
it scrubs off the dust of not-seeing,

and I see her sandals, black like mine,
and I see her dress, white like mine.
Little by little, she comes clear.
She rises up in a skin of water.

As long as the water shines, I can see her.
As long as I see her, we can play
by the light of the moon on my bed,
by the light of the stars on my bear
till the sun opens its eye, the sun that wakes things,
the sun that doesn't believe in ghosts . . .

NANCY WILLARD